The Water Shed

by

SUZANNE MADRON

Acknowledgements: A huge thank you to D. Alexander Ward for motivating me to write not one, but two stories. Long live King Wasp and Spider Grrl.

Author Note: Hello, friends and readers. If you have ever known a childhood fear, you know how it clings to you through the years. My fears as a child centered around an out-of-place dilapidated shed in the middle of an overgrown hay field and a golden apple tree.

This story is about the shed.

Author pages:

Suzanne Madron:

https://www.facebook.com/SuzanneMadron

Website:

https://sites.google.com/view/suzanne-madron/

Additional works by Suzanne Madron can be found on Amazon.com

The Water Shed

By

Suzanne Madron

The building stood off-kilter and out-of-place in the middle of a disheveled field of wild hay on a remote part of the property, but to say it was lost in the one hundred and eight acre former farmstead was not true. Somehow the warped planks, disguised as they were by masks of lichen and a wall of long-dead wild raspberry brambles, were obvious even from a distance, like a shipwreck sticking out of the sand of an abandoned beach.

As children, my cousins and I had been forbidden to explore the structure. There were many dilapidated buildings on the property, but only two areas were completely off-limits. The first was the part of the barn that had been struck by lightning around half a century ago, the boards still black and reeking of fire and smoke on humid days. The water shed was the second restricted place, with its gaping window and collapsing walls.

At one point, it had been used for irrigation, but that was long before our time. Water from an underground aquifer filled a cistern that was more a dangerous, jagged square cut into the ground and built up in corroded metal than the well it was intended to be. From the outside of the building we were unable to see into the reservoir. All we could see from our nervous glances through the broken-out and sagging window frame was the attempt to cover the open well with bowed, rotten boards weighed down with masonry.

Somewhere in the field on the slope below the water shed there was supposed to have been a valve which had allowed an irrigation system to be hooked up in order to drain the cistern without having to go near the water shed itself, as if the original owners of the property also felt the odd sense of foreboding surrounding the place. We never found the valve, and assumed it had been buried long ago.

We didn't question our parents' orders not to explore the building. There was something about the shed that suggested it didn't *want* anyone to go inside, that there was something dark and hungry in there. It was a subterranean thing as old as the aquifer beneath the cistern. Even on the sunniest of days the hayfield in which the water shed stood was gloomy and uninviting, with a lone, twisted, ancient apple tree to stand sentinel at the edge of where the lawn ended and the field began.

Decades had passed since those childhood summer afternoons had been turned cold by the dare from one of my cousins to get next to the water shed, to *touch it*. A lifetime had gone by since the sounds from inside the structure had sent us screaming in terror that last hot afternoon, and we hadn't ventured near it since. My family had moved shortly after the incident, leaving the property and all its ghosts behind in our wake.

Until today.

I stood on the edge of the overgrown yard and stared in disbelief across the field gone wild with years of orchard grass. There it was, still standing as if by some dark miracle. The old, gray planks making up the walls were just as I remembered them, and the dead raspberry brambles looked as sharp and thorny as they had been in my youth. I knew that to move through them would be like scaling a fence topped in razor wire while wearing no clothes. Once again I stared into the cyclopean, heavy-lidded window and shivered.

"Dare you to touch it."

I was too tired to feel the terror I should have felt at the words and I turned to stare at my cousin John. He tried to smile, but his amusement quickly faded as his eyes lingered on the water shed lurking in the distance. Time had taken its toll on him and his hair was now gray at the temples, his expression haggard. He looked as if he hadn't slept in years. I wondered if any of us had slept a full night since that last summer.

"Dare *you* to touch it," I countered, but it was an empty threat. I took out a pack of cigarettes from my jacket pocket and opened it.

Neither one of us smiled.

"OK. Why the hell are we here?"

John and I turned as the eldest of my cousins approached us. His dark suit had been neatly pressed and his hair was a pure and silvery white slicked back from his face. He looked at us with ice-blue eyes the color of dead things trapped beneath frozen water.

"I got a call from my mother," I told them. "So?"

I wasn't looking to see who had bothered to ask the question, or if it had been both of them in unison. It didn't matter. I tapped a cigarette out of the pack. The lighter flame shook as I held it to the cigarette clenched between my teeth, but I was able to get the damned thing lit after the third try. "*After* she died."

My cousin John shivered. "OK, creepy. You sure it was her?"

I nodded.

He rubbed the back of his neck and let out a shaking breath. "Ghost calls aside, what's that got to do with this place?"

"She called from the old number. *This* number. She said she was here." My voice cracked. "She said she was scared. I already checked every other building here, but I couldn't do the water shed alone." I grimaced at the admission, but my cousins' faces said they understood.

John shuddered and looked away. At least he believed me. I had a hard time not thinking I was insane.

"Shoulda sold this place a long time ago," Larry muttered, glaring across the field. His eyes became unfocused as they fell on the water shed; he hadn't been listening. "Now that the place is yours, what are you going to do with *that*?" He jutted his chin toward the old shed and sneered.

"I'm not sure yet." I shook out two more cigarettes and handed them to my cousins and passed around the lighter. "I have to figure out how bad the cistern is and what it'll take to just tear the thing down."

John ran a hand through his graying hair. "Place still makes my skin crawl."

I nodded and said nothing. For years I had assumed we'd sold off the property, but discovered the decision of who would pull the plug had been a grudge match between my parents for the last couple of decades. My father had wanted to keep it, my mother had wanted to leave, and an argument had ensued. As a result, in true stubborn married couple fashion, neither of them would budge, and out of spite, neither of them had created a real estate listing.

The property had sat vacant and running wild for the better part of twenty years. I didn't know how it had ended up in my mother's name, or why she had passed it to me when she died. Perhaps to get the final word in now that my father was too old to keep the place up by himself, or maybe because she knew I would sell it. Whatever her reasons had been, I had avoided doing anything with it for months after she died until the day the call came.

Something strange happens when loved ones pass, and we tend to hold onto scraps of them — anything we have — including an old phone number. I couldn't explain how I remembered it, but when the phone rang and the operator asked to connect the old number, I didn't hesitate. Then I heard my mother's voice patched through.

Her words were filled with static and fading in and out across the line. In a panic I moved closer to the receiver, as if it could strengthen the connection.

"Where are you?" she asked. There was an odd reverberating hiss in the background, as if she stood in a large empty room.

"I'm here, Mom. Where are *you*?"

"At the old house, but no one else is here. Where is everyone? Sam, I'm scared."

There was a loud crackle followed by a click, then silence. I wanted to scream, but mostly I cried. It was the sobbing, ugly cry of a lost child. My mother was at the old house, and I needed to help her.

I never told my father about the phone call. Instead, I wrote to my cousins telling them to meet me at the old house.

As the three of us stood there smoking our cigarettes and staring across the field, a wind carrying the chill of autumn blew around us. The huge, old pine trees surrounding one corner of the property by the road sighed in the breeze. It was a sound that always reminded me of Halloween.

Larry was the first to break the brittle silence. "Why'd you write us, Sam?"

I took a deep drag off my cigarette and wondered if I could flick the glowing stick far enough into the field of dry grass to burn down the old gray building. "I needed someone here with me to check the water shed for Mom, to make sure she's not in there, and you're the only ones who know what really happened that last day we went up there." I took a steadying breath. "I needed someone to go for help in case…"

"We were just children!" John's voice cracked and his eyes never left the gray structure in the field.

"Yes, we were. Which is why we're here now, to settle this, and to help Mom." I took another drag off my cigarette and started across the field.

"What the hell are you doing?"

"As crazy as it might sound, I need to make sure my mother's not in there. I'm also hoping to get some damned closure so I can sleep through the night for once." I turned to face my cousins, walking backward across the field. "I'm tired. Aren't you?"

Larry and John looked at one another, then back to me. Larry started across the field toward me.

"Wait, I'm coming."

"This is insane," John called after us. "There wasn't anything in there when we were kids, and there's nothing in there now!"

I smirked back at him. "Then come on. *Dare you to touch it.*"

John growled. "Fine." He started across the field toward us. "Dare you to touch the *cistern.*"

"Fine."

It was slow going. The tall grass at the edges of the field had been matted into sleeping spaces by deer in some places, and had become tangled and windblown in others. As we drew nearer to the old water shed, the grass wrapped around our legs as if to pull us back from our destination, but we continued on, determined to end decades of nightmares.

We kept moving, our conversation dying as we looked up the hill to the water shed. It seemed larger than I remembered, and I expected crows to take flight from around it as we came closer.

"When the hell did it get so dark?" John asked with sudden panic.

We looked up at the sky and I felt a sinking in the pit of my stomach. The wind had blown a storm in across the mountain, and I cursed myself for not remembering how fast storms moved through the place when I was a kid.

"Let's get this over with."

We walked around the building in search of a door, but there was none. The only access point was the lopsided window.

"Who built this thing?" John asked, running a hand through his hair.

"I don't know, and I don't care." I stepped on the brambles and mashed them to the ground, then knocked out the jagged panes of the window with my elbow. The grayed wood fell, still holding its shape of a crooked cross as it hit the floor inside the water shed in a spray of broken glass.

Leaning into the opening, I tested the structure to ensure we wouldn't be buried in old boards when we ventured into the shed. It was oddly flexible, yet solid. I took a look around inside the building and noted the lack of vegetation in spite of the hole in the roof over the cistern.

The floor was a mess of crumbling concrete that was half-buried beneath rotted strips of tarpaper and splinters from the collapsed roof. In the middle of the shed was the old cistern, the metal sides corroded and standing roughly waist-high. The boards once covering the opening had fallen into the well long ago, leaving the cistern open to the elements and any unsuspecting wildlife.

I peered into the well and shuddered. The water was a milky grayish white, the fallen boards black and decaying in the water. I could see claw marks lining the metal walls where animals had fallen in and failed to climb back out.

"Sam, come out of there. I don't like this," John whispered from the window.

It felt as if time had reversed, and we were kids again. My heart pounded in my chest so loudly I could hardly hear Larry's voice from outside the water shed.

"What are these markings? Do either of you remember these marks up here? I've never seen anything like them." He paused, and I could see him in my mind's eye, touching the marks he had found.

I was leaning over the cistern, staring into the water. "Mom?" I whispered so the others wouldn't hear me.

There was something floating down there, but I couldn't see it well enough in the fading light from the darkening sky. I leaned further over the edge of the cistern, feeling the metal lip cut into my waist, and held my lighter into the well. About fifteen feet below the meager light from the flame, something with an odd shape that my mind refused to grasp was submerged next to one of the fallen boards.

"There's something down there," I called out.

John shifted nervously outside the window. "It's probably some poor animal. Come *on*, Sam, your mother's gone. She's not in there!"

"I think we should go."

I had never heard Larry's voice sound so unsure, scared even. I looked toward the window and the sky was black now. The wind whipped over the field, blowing John's hair into his face as he stared wide-eyed at the sky.

"What is it?"

John shook his head, unable to speak as he pointed upward. I heard Larry crunching through dead underbrush as he ran toward the window.

He stuck his face in and his skin was ashen. "We have to go. NOW."

I looked at the sky through the hole in the roof, and could see the dark clouds moving in a slow, angry circle.

"Shit!"

"Is that what I think it is?" John yelled over the howling wind.

"Not waiting to find out!" My words were ripped from my mouth as the wind picked up. The clouds overhead had formed into an ominous upside down cone, and the point reached toward the earth just past the tree line.

John and Larry started to run back toward the main building, and I jumped through the open window to follow. When we had lived there, the building had been a hotel and restaurant, but now the windows to the upper floors were broken, the paint peeling away in flypaper strips. Lightning struck the rods lining the roof, giving the place a foreboding, Gothic air. I was already fumbling the keys out of my pocket as we hit the door, and the entryway protected us from the wind enough to catch our breath.

I shoved the key into the lock and in moments we were inside and rushing for the basement. The space wasn't huge, and had been used as storage for most of our tenure. It was built of old fieldstone, with a dirt floor that stayed cool in the summer and a heavy wooden door with hinges that protested moving after being idle for so long.

There was no electricity. It had been turned off long ago, and the pipes had been winterized before the last of the family moved out. The stoves and ovens could still work, if the gas tank outside still had gas left in it, but other than that, we were on our own.

I dug through the scraps along the back wall, wondering if any candles had been left behind. I found an old kerosene lantern buried on a back shelf and gave it a shake. The sound of liquid sloshing inside greeted me and I lit it with a sigh of relief. The light was dim, but enough to see by once our eyes had adjusted to the darkness.

The small windows toward the top of the basement would have provided ample light on any other day, but the sky was far too dark for that now. Through the grime-covered windows, we could see up the hill toward the water shed and make out its dark outline in stark contrast to the glowing hay surrounding it.

"Aren't we supposed to block the windows if there's a tornado?" Larry asked.

I shrugged. "Never been through one, so I have no clue."

We looked to John, and he stared up the hill at the water shed. He didn't say anything, and he didn't have to. We followed his gaze and a chill ran down my spine.

The funnel cloud that had begun forming over our heads was now a fully formed tornado moving through the field. Bolts of lightning reached out like fingers, digging into the ground around the water shed. From inside the building came an odd greenish glow, like foxfire.

I reached to open the small basement window so I could see better. It was a hinged affair that swung inward and up when open, and the locks were rusty. I had to struggle with them, but finally managed to pull it free and it creaked on its hinges as I pushed it upward.

"Get away from the window!" Larry shouted, and tried to hold me back.

I shrugged him off and we gathered around the open window, propping it up with an old brick. The light show on the hill was even more dazzling now, and the eldritch glow inside the water shed was growing brighter and brighter.

"What the hell is it?" John asked.

None of us answered. We had no idea.

A shadow began to move within the old shed, its form pitch black against the green glow as it climbed out of the old cistern on long, oddly jointed legs. A flash of lightning lit the inside of the shed for the briefest of moments and I screamed.

The thing in the water shed came to attention, as if it could hear me even over the noise of the storm, and it leapt through the hole in the roof. John and Larry clapped their hands over my mouth and wrestled me to the dirt floor of the basement.

"Put out that light and cover the windows!" Larry hissed and John moved to comply.

As my cousin moved through the basement blocking off the windows he turned and looked at us. "Did anyone lock the door behind us?"

Larry fished through my pockets and threw the keys to John. "Do it!"

John left us and as soon as he was sure I wouldn't scream, Larry continued the tasks he had given to John. I watched him, numb with shock, as he closed the small window and locked it, then began stuffing old cardboard over the glass.

"Did you see it?" I asked him, my voice barely a whisper.

"No."

"You had to have seen it."

He looked at me, and his eyes flickered like flames in the lamplight. "I didn't see anything, and you didn't see anything either. To remember it is to summon it, so don't think about it."

John rushed back into the storage area and slammed the door behind him. He began piling anything he could find against the door, his eyes wild with terror. "It's outside!" he whispered.

"Outside?" Larry glared at him. "Where outside? You mean inside?"

"I mean *outside*! I saw it moving around the building when I locked the door. Jesus it's huge!"

"Stop talking about it!" Larry hissed. "I'm putting out the lamp. We have to stay silent."

He blew out the flame and we were entombed in darkness. From outside, we could hear the howl of the tornado moving across the field and we huddled together. The floor trembled beneath us, and we waited. From the entryway, we heard the sound of crashing glass and splintering wood, the crumbling of fieldstone as the front porch was torn free.

The sound was like a freight train screaming through, and we leaned against the wall, steeling ourselves for the worst. It was over in minutes that felt like days, and the silence left in its wake was worse than the tornado itself. It felt as if my eardrums would rupture from the lack of sound.

Then sound returned, and it was worse than the storm. From out of the darkness came scraping nails over concrete flooring. *Clack clack, clack clack.* Getting closer and closer. At last, whatever creature making the noise was there outside the storage room door. The lock jiggled, and claws searched across the wood planks for a point of entry.

I was transported back to childhood, to the dare at the water shed. *Dare you to touch it.* We had touched it, each of us, and woke whatever horrible thing slept in the depths of that cistern.

As John met the challenge we heard that same scraping sound along the inside wall of the water shed, moving toward the window.

As we sat there now, huddled in the dark, we knew that same thing I had seen climbing out of the cistern in the water shed, was back to finish what had begun decades ago. We heard the lock rattle again, more insistent this time, the scratching against the door more aggressive. The sound of wood breaking was a gunshot in the dark.

"We have to get out of here," I whispered.

"How?" John asked.

"Through the windows."

"But the storm…"

"To hell with the storm, it's better than whatever is out there trying to get in."

We stood up and leaned boxes against the wall, moving as quickly and silently as we could while outside the door the thing picked apart the wooden planks. We propped the window open and Larry was the first one to go through, being the strongest. John was next, then me.

Behind me I expected the door to come crashing down into the room and the thing beyond to tear me apart. But I slid through the window and removed the brick, letting it fall to the floor before silently closing the glass.

The sky swirled above us, and I could see more funnel clouds forming around the eye of the storm. We had to head back up the hill, I realized. It was where we had parked.

We scaled the hill in a rush, passing by the water shed as we raced the storm. When we reached the flattened parking area, my stomach lurched. The cars were gone. In their places were masses of twisted metal torn apart by the tornado that had touched down. I glared at the field, at the split apple tree and the untouched planks of the water shed.

"What the hell are we going to do?" John screamed.

Larry frowned down at us. "Come with me."

He led us up the slope toward the water shed and John balked. He shook his head and began backing toward the tree line.

"Get back here!"

"No! I'm not going near that thing. I saw what Sam saw!"

Larry pursed his lips and took a swing at our younger cousin. The blow connected with the side of John's head and he went sprawling into the grass. Larry looked at me and arched an eyebrow.

"You coming, or do I need to calm you down, too?"

"Why are you doing this?" My mouth had gone dry, and my mind was running in a million directions as I tried to figure out a way to save John and escape.

"We were never supposed to leave that day," he told me as he dragged John through the field. As if sensing my own impending flight, he grabbed me by the arm and pulled me with him as he made his way up the hill. "The marks on the shed? I could read them after I touched them, and they showed me…"

"What did they show you?"

"That we were supposed to die that day." He nodded toward the water shed and his eyes were glazed with rapture. "In there...down deep, in the darkwater."

"No we weren't, that's crazy." I tugged my arm free and shoved Larry.

He stumbled over John's unconscious form as I ran back down the slope. I almost made it to where the cars had been when he tackled me to the ground.

"This is for your own good, Sam."

I stared up at him in disbelief, at the rock held in his hand. The darkness was quick and all-encompassing as he brought it down on the side of my head.

There was a splash and I woke with a start. I had no idea how much time had passed, but the storm was beginning to blow again as the eye moved over us. Cold water tasting of a wet basement and rotting flesh filled my mouth and I flapped against it, sputtering. There was a second splash next to me and in the dim light I could see the shape was human.

"John?"

No answer. I looked up and saw a square of light fifteen feet above with the dark outline of a head and shoulders cutting into the lines. I pulled John's head out of the water, but he wasn't breathing, and there was no pulse at his throat.

"Larry! Pull us out! I think John's…"

Larry's mad laughter, as it echoed off the cistern walls, left me cold. There was a loud scratching noise I could make out even over the wind. It came from the walls of the cistern as I sensed something climb up out of the water next to me.

Larry's silhouette was jerked away from the edge of the well and then he was screaming. The sound was abruptly cut off seconds later, leaving me alone with the storm and the thing that had risen out of the depths. I held onto John's body and used it as a float. I wasn't sure how deep the cistern was, but I knew it was enough to drown me.

The click of claws on concrete drew my attention upward. Blackness filled the fading square of light and I was pushed beneath the murky water as something splashed down on top of me. I kicked and shoved my way free from it, escaping heavy limbs and teeth as it sank, then bobbed back to the surface. I heard the creature above me as it moved around the cistern, its steps quick and eager.

I reached out to the thing bobbing next to me in the water and felt the remnants of a silk tie. I reached up toward the face and could feel the gash at Larry's throat, the open scream still stretching wide his dead mouth. In my head I could hear Larry's voice, taunting, *Dare you to touch it.*

Above me, I could hear the sound of something scraping over the edge of the cistern as the last of the light faded, leaving me in darkness. The stench of the cistern and the thing that lived in it was unbearable, and as it bore down on me I reached out a hand to touch its wretched form. As my fingers slid across the slimy flesh, a phone rang beneath the water.

The End

Author's Endnote

The water shed itself, while based on a faded memory from my childhood, was also quite real and a piece of farm history. Of that property's history. The place had been left uninhabited for a bit before my family bought it and started to restore it. Parts of old systems were still in place and still working long after they should have been replaced, but if it's not broke…. One of those systems still in place was the water shed.

We did eventually manage to get inside the old building. It seemed huge to me, even though it was probably only a shack. I'm sure my father's head brushed the jagged boards of the collapsing ceiling.

The cistern was very real and I remember it was filled with a milky, murky water. In my memory, there was even a heap of fur sprawled soggy and wet on a bit of fallen-in roof down in that well. I was never sure what the animal was, or even if it was an animal at all, but over the years I imagined it as a woodchuck, a raccoon, and a giant rat. In my nightmares I would see it struggling to climb the walls of the metal cistern, the oxidation crumbling away in its paws/claws.

After moving away, it was years before I even thought about the water shed. I wrote a few scary stories based on ghosts and vampires and forgot all about the water shed and its secrets.

While thinking about writing a submission for the *Shadows Over Main Street, Volume 2* anthology, I remembered a nightmare I had had about Adirondack chairs (don't ask, I have no idea) and the field they had been in. It was the same field as the water shed. The old unease came creeping back as an insidious tingle at the base of my mind until it emerged like a monster from a murky old farm cistern hidden away in a falling-down building.

I started to write and before I knew it, I had a story. Some of the pieces are from memories of long ago, expanded to fit adult sizes and shapes. Other bits are completely made up. Either way, I hope you've enjoyed the story and look forward to seeing you in future pages.

~ Suzi

Additional Works by Suzanne Madron

Apocrypha of the Apocalypse

Second-Hand Sarah

The Immortal War Series

Nemesis

Lamia

The Tower

Scylla

A God in a House of Crosses

The Metatron Mysteries

The Murdered Metatron

The Dispossessed

The Resurrectionist

Novellas and Short Stories

For Sale or Rent

Unseen

The Cat with Cthulhu Eyes

Blood in the Water

Love Notes

www.ingramcontent.com/pod-product-compliance
Lightning Source LLC
Chambersburg PA
CBHW071256130726
47998CB00003B/1211